THE ECLIPSE

SAHIL SAHOO

Made with ♥ on the Notion Press Platform
www.notionpress.com

Contents

Prologue

Cairo, Egpyt

   (2 months earlier)

"Your Majesty, we've recently recieved some news." a man stood nervously, as nervous as an acrobat on a wobbly wire.

"News." a lavish man repeated while gazing at his splendid watch, adorned with diamonds and emeralds.

"What is this *news*, Lieutenant?"

"Orion has disappeared."

Vesper Nightshade, the leader of a hidden society located in the heart of Cairo, took of his dark glasses, revealing a crescent shaped scar on his left eye.

"Any information of his whereabouts?" Vesper asked.

"He was last seen off the coast of Santa Monica Beach. It seems that he was after the Annihilator. He launched his blackhole as planned, but it seems that there was a resistance, and he got locked in the area through the portal."

Vesper pounded his fist on the table in fury, making his Lieutenant wince in fear. "The Secrecy bet us to the Annihilator! We'll have to accelerate our plans Lieutenant."

"It wasn't mostly The Secrecy, your Majesty. It was a group of gen-twos and kids: Austin and Destiny Sanders, Jack Sanders, and Julius Benny."

Vesper's brow knitted into a perplexed frown. "Who?"

"Austin has telekinetic powers, whereas Destiny has short flight capability. Juliu-"

"Telekinesis?!" Vesper questioned. "It's been a long time since one with such powerful abilities.", silence filled in the awkward gap as Vesper glanced at the lush carpet, thinking of a plan.

"It's time, Lieutenant. Notify the crew to increase security around The Arcane, and get the special and stealth forces ready."

"Yes, your Majesty. But from my sources, it seems that the force of Austin's team is stronger than we think. I suggest we charge soon! " the Lieutenant recommended. Vesper thought about the request.

"Your right. If this "*Austin*" kid defeated Orion, I believe its time. But, the Secrecy is first, Lieutenant. If it doesn't work, we always have the Shadow Scepter."

"Yes. We have the Scepter."

I Almost Get Killed By Sand

April 1st is usually a day when people revel in pranks and laughter. A day full of hilarious jokes, and a day full of prank calls. Normal kids might swap salt for sugar or hide whoopee cushions on chairs. But my April 1st? Well, let's just say it was a bit "*out of the ordinary*".

If you haven't come across my first adventure, well... pleased to meet you: I'm Austin Sanders, I'm 13, I live in California, and I love heavy metal rock and pizza. Oh yeah, and I also have a little knack for moving objects with my mind. Don't believe me? Well, you might have heard about a certain "500-year-old monument going down in flames."*Well...* that might have been my doing. My twin, Destiny can fly, my friend Julius can go invisible, and there is a whole society called "The Secrecy" with people with powers like this. Two months ago, we got hunted by the police, had an epic car chase, stopped an evil dude named Orion. He had space-controlling powers, and he nearly destroyed the planet using a supreme weapon called "The Annihilator" that amplified his powers by tenfold.

Luckily, we locked him somewhere no one can reach, and now we got invited by the Secrecy to spend our spring break in their hideout, but tensions are rising.

That's the whole story. Still kind of skeptical? Well, here's the next story. Decide for yourself. It all started when we fought gloriously against sand.

The situation was simple: visit the Secrecy for the first time, attend a few training sessions for our powers, and attend the grand celebration of defeating Orion. It might sound exciting, but first, me and Destiny had to get through the hard part: finding a hidden society that has been, well, hidden for centuries.

Uncle Leo and our cousin Jack decided to help us find it, but it wasn't looking great after a few hours of driving in the desert.

"Ugh! It's been hours! Are we there yet? And are you even sure that piece of junk even works? 'Cause if it doesn't, I wil-" Destiny mumbled, her dark hair blowing back in her face.

"Could you stop talking for once? The crystal should work and it's glowing a lot, so we should be there soon." I interrupted her. I played with a pink crystal in my hand. It was about the size of my palm and glowed a bright blue. Julius had given it to me, saying "It will glow brighter when you get closer to the Secrecy." Right now, it was glowing slightly, which wasn't a good sign considering that we had been roaming for nearly 4 hours.

Our plan wasn't looking good.

I gazed outside, watching over the vast desert, looking for a sign. The sun painted the sky in splashes of pink and yellow, and it was starting to get dark.

"Are there usually tornadoes in the desert?" Jack asked randomly, staring out the car window.

"I guess there are sandstorms occasionally. Why-" Uncle Leo started but paused midway. "Oh my."

Uncle Leo's face wore a grave expression, sending chills down my spine. I frantically scanned the area, and there it was. 2 swirling sand tornadoes around the height of a palm tree, zoomed towards us. Taking in tons of sand from its surroundings, the tornadoes destroyed everything in their path. And it seemed as if they were coming right towards us.

Uncle Leo drifted the car to a stop and we jumped out of the car. Shaking in panic, we all ran towards a small dune that was not in the tornadoes' path. However, just as we reached the dune, the tornadoes changed direction and started to move towards us. I scanned the tornado, and at that moment, my jaw dropped to the ground.

"They aren't tornadoes! They're people!" I yelled.

Like real-life mummies, the two people wore some kind of linen clothing that covered their whole body. Unfazed from the chaos around them, they moved their hands in a circle at the same time, and the sand beneath them began to rise, creating a colossal sand golem! Its eyes had a wicked dark orange glint, and it eyed us like its prey.

"RUN!" Destiny shouted.

Its sandy fist plumetted towards Destiny, but in the nick of time, she flew away. The golem's towered above us, everyone of its steps sending waves of sand and debris towards us. I could barely move a step.

We had to think fast. I gazed around in the soulless dunes, the heat boiling me alive. A humongous green cactus caught my eye, and I concentrated on it. I focused all of my telekinesis on it and tried to make it budge, but time was running out and nothing was happening. The sand golem hid us in its shadow, and was about to crush me in its sandy grip.

Using all my strength, the cactus finally floated into the air. In the nick of time, I hauled the cactus towards the golem. Suddenly, I heard a loud growl. The golem disintegrated, and this time it didn't grow back. A huge wave of sand from the golem knocked the mummy-people off their feet. Before they could get back up, I hauled the cactus again towards them. Uncle Leo sighed in relief, but even he knew there wasn't any time. We sprinted towards the mummy-people and we examined them, trying to find out who they were. Spikes surrounded their body, and they looked like porcupines.

"Throwing a cactus at them was quite harsh," Jack muttered and then smirked. "Wait, does it say 'Secrecy' on their headband?"

The word "Secrecy" beamed on their bandanas, glowing a weak purple.

"We're guards!", one of the mummy-people said faintly.

Our eyes widened open. Of course. They were the guards of the Secrecy, and I had just thrown a cactus towards them.

Destiny shot back, "Who are the little kids now, huh?! Wait, the crystal is glowing a lot!"

I stared at the crystal in my hand, and sure enough, it was beaming with a blue glow.

"It's near here, maybe we can squeeze out the location from the guards." Uncle Leo suggested while slumping on a hill of sand. Suddenly, we heard a metal clang. He dusted off some sand and there it was: a thick metal door with a blank screen.

"You can't get through it though! The key was with me, but now it's destroyed. Might as well go back home now!", one of the guards said with a smug face. Pierced with a spike, the keycard was obliterated and the small flicker of hope we had was crushed. I banged the door in fury. All of our effort was for nothing. Anger and rage fueled my body and I focused my energy on the door. If I couldn't open the door with the key, I was going to open the door my way. My telekinesis surged, and I concentrated all my might on the door. Screws flew out, and with a resounding crash, the door slammed onto the sandy ground. The room beyond was engulfed in darkness, concealing its secrets.

"That was quick." Jack remarked. "Welp, see ya later guards!"

Me, Jack, Destiny, and Uncle Leo stepped into the darkness, and we couldn't believe what happened next.

CHAPTER TWO

A Sword-Head Welcomes Us

As soon as we lurked past the door, a few beams of lights flickered above us. The metal ground beneath us swayed, and before I realized it was an elevator, it jolted down. Like rusty gears turning in a machine, a discordant grinding sound echoed through the lift, bouncing off the walls and booming in our ears. If this was how the headquarter's lift was like, I was already regretting spending 10 hours coming here to spend my time in a old garbage bin. After it came to an abrupt stop, a noxic wave of nausea washed over me, making me gag. The smell of oil ignited my senses, making me alarmed. After what seemed like years, the door finally opened, revealing a tall well-dressed man.

His tuxedo caught my eye, but what astonished me more was what was above his tuxedo.

"Woah! Your head is a sword!" I exclaimed.

"Well technically, I can change it to whatever I want!" the man said. He then proceeded to change his appearance to Jack!

"That's sick!" Jack said with enthusiasm. "It's like looking in a mirror! How do you do that"

After changing back to a fancy "normal" man, he said "You must be Austin, Destiny, Jack, and Mr Leo. My name's Axel, and the president of the Secrecy has asked me to show you around!" The man said. He wore glasses that covered his eyebrows, and his extravagant tuxedo blocked our view.

"As for you Jack, I'm a master shapeshifter. But more importantly, I will be your butler for your stay." Axel said.

"Welcome to your home for this week."

He shifted to the side, and what we saw next was wonderful. It was a giant white hall, filled with vibrant art and lights.

"WOAH!" Destiny exclaimed. "That's cool!"

It was truly amazing! As we walked, we noticed laboratories filled with focused scientists, rooms filled with people with powers training (which excited me a lot), and last but not least, a beautiful banquet hall filled with a small grandiose stage, and stunning chairs and tables.

Scientists eyed us, like we were a precious gem, and people all over stopped what they were doing just to stare at us.

"Is there something on my face?" Destiny asked, as if she could read my mind.

Axel laughed heartily, and replied "You all are kind of like a celebrity here. Everyone is excited to meet all of you, as no new powered people have appeared in a long time."

"How long?" Uncle Leo asked.

"500 years." Axel replied.

Everyone of our eyes widened. It made me happy, knowing that I was so special. But deep down, it stung me, and I knew that under this facade of admiration, there would be a burden for being different.

"Is that for the party?" Jack asked, pointing to the banquet, changing the subject.

"Yes. But trust me, it's more than just a party." Axel replied, making me smile in excitement.

Axel guided us to yet another elevator, but it was much better than the last one. Then, we went to our rooms, passing by the food canteen. From decadent muffins, to pancakes, the wafts from the canteen made my mouth water.

"The people here are very friendly, you will have no problems fitting in!" Axel assured us, while still guiding us to our rooms.

"Well, your two guards were really friendly." I said, while rolling my eyes. "They literally attacked us for no reason!"

"Ah. I see you've already met Kylo and Drake. They're one of our most talented sand elementalists, and they're twins, as well as guards. As for attacking you, well.. your arrival was slightly unexpected. The Secrecy has been undergoing some issues." Axel said.

Silence filled the hall. What issues? And if it heavily affected a society with superpowers, how big was the issue?

"But not to worry. Ah, we've reached your rooms. Go for it!"

I stared in awe at 4 doors, with gold handles and a sweet smell.

"Dibs!" Jack yelled while pushing me aside. He opened door, and bolted inside.

Joining in, I ran towards another room, and a beautiful sight unfolded before me. There was a fluffy white bed, a massive TV, and a bathroom that looked like it could have parked a car!

I looked outside my window, where the sandy winds covered the starry night sky. This was way too good to be true.

CHAPTER THREE

I Eavesdrop With a Butterknife

That night I had the craziest dream.

I was stuck in a dark room, on a dark chair, with dark shadows draining my energy, like some sort of parasite. All my limbs were frozen, and I couldn't say anything.

However, a loud thunderclap woke me up from that dream, and I decided not to think about it that much.

As soon as I thought my imagination was done playing tricks on me, I heard footsteps and murmurs outside. I checked my watch groggily, and it was 2:00 a.m.

Would I get in trouble if I sneaked out?

Sure I would.

Was my curiousity bigger than my fear?

A hundred percent.

I grabbed a butterknife: my only defense if things went awry, and tiptoed out of the room.

I walked further along the hallway. There was no sound of footsteps. Or talking. I shook it off as just some "late-night-after-nightmare-hallucination", and walked back to my room. But right before I went in, I saw a shadow. It was in a turn in the hallway, but every nerve of my body warned me not to go.

What did I do, you may ask?

I went to the edge of the hallway, and heard 2 people talking.

I couldn't get a good look at them, but they were mumbling something that I could barely understand.

"(....) aren't ready yet. We can't risk them knowing this early. It will only make things worse." a voice whispered.

I recognized the voice almost immediately. It belonged to Axel.

"The eclipse is nearing already, and the last time it happened, you know the complications." the other woman said.

Complications? A shiver ran down my spine.

"Last time we were able to fend them off. " Axel started, but suddenly a cold hand went over my mouth. My whole body became alarmed because, well, I couldn't see the hand. And then I realized who it was.

"Hey. I thought you weren't an eavesdropper." I heard a voice. My brows shot up as I recognized him.

"Julius! Well, I wouldn't be eavesdropping if it wasn't important. And covering my mouth is pretty annoying." I said.

Julius became visible, and his smile eased my fear.

I had first met Julius last year in a random shack in the middle of nowhere. Me, Destiny, and my cousin Jack had found him after escaping the police, and we saw him on the news. After offering us a ride and helping us defeat Orion, a villain attempting to destroy the world with the Annihilator, we've been friends since. Although I haven't seen him in a while after he returned back to the Secrecy,

"It isn't that bad... but it's scheduled to be during the party. And unlike last time it isnt a partial solar eclipse. It's a total one. Who knows how much stronger they'll be this time?" the woman said.

Solar eclipses? A grave feeling gnawed on my insides. Who was going to invade the Secrecy, and what were they going to do?

As if Julius could read my mind, he whispered, "2 years ago, during an eclipse, a loud alarm randomly started ringing in the middle of the night. And the eclipse after that, and after that. Its been a running joke that there was a monster that came during the eclipse just to set off the alarm. Well I guess we weren't that far off."

"Whatever it is, I'm sure they'll have it under control. I've never really liked parties anyways." I muttered. We went back to eavesdropping.

"The total eclipse is nearing Axel, do you know what could happen during an eclipse, I guess all we can do is increase the security around floor 5?"

Floor 5? I mean the level was off limits, so I had always wondered what could've been up there. And that's when Julius nudged me, and my butterknife fell on the floor, making a ringing noise that echoed through the hallway. The woman and Axel immediately stopped their conversation. I turned around to Julius with glaring eyes, but he was already tiptoeing away.

"Just go invisible!" I said, tiptoeing quickly towards him.

"How about you?"

"I'll figure something out!"

"Alright good luck" Julius said before disappearing and running away

I smacked my head, and I could tell they were coming towards us.

"Run!"

We quickly sneaked backwards, slowly closing my door. I jumped onto my bed, and thought about what I just heared. My powers could be going next. Or Destiny's. This was terrible. However, the following night, things took a turn for the worst.

CHAPTER FOUR

SHADOWS CRASH A PARTY

If there's one thing I hate more than getting news that your life might turn upside down, it's parties. But this party was like no other. Tables lined the whole area with various food, and colorful lights lit up the surroundings while Secrecy members mingled in clusters, their faces partially covered by creepy masks, chattering. Although I have lots of food allergies, I could still appreciate the glorious spread of food in the party. From hot dogs stalls to

Suddenly, the lights dimmed and a deafening silence emerged throughout the party area; not your typical party. Me, Jack, and Destiny sat down in one of the chairs and Axel appeared on the stage with his human form. I almost forgot he was the secretary's president, but something troubled me. He was wearing the same expression that he wore last night.

"Welcome everybody. I hope you all are enjoying our little party that we have set up. It's been a long time since the whole Secrecy has come together to enjoy a night, so I hope you all are having a good time so far!" Axel exclaimed while tapping his finger nervously on his shirt.

Nothing bad yet, I thought to myself. I scanned the crowd for Julius, but couldn't find him over the waves of seats and people that filled the party hall.

"I'm sorry to have to interrupt this party, but there are some pressing matters that must be discussed immediately. As some of you may have heard, some members of the Secrecy have been experiencing... power fluctuations. If this continues, at this rate, everyone's powers will be obsolete by the end of the month."

Panicking murmurs broke the silence. A deep feeling gnawed deep inside my chest. By the end of the month? Even I began to panic. Destiny gave a grave expression as well, and I knew she was thinking the same thing. Twin mentality I guess.

"We are working on a way to restore them but until then there's no need to panic yet. On the other hand, let's welcome in two new part-time members of the Secrecy who have come here after helping us defeat Orion. Let's give a warm welcome to Austin and Destiny!"

Claps erupted from the Secrecy, and although I appreciated it, my mind clung to what Axel had said. But what happened next changed everything.

From the sides of the stage, wispy dark smoke started flooding the party while massive, scary shadows emerged from the ground.

"What's that?" Jack whispered. The whole Secrecy started stirring and running around as panic settled down on the Secrecy. I was confident that the Secrecy could beat a bunch of shadows, but without their powers, we were doomed. The shadows were not ordinary either: instead of clinging onto surfaces, these shadows stood in the air. However, I could faintly make out something.

The shadows resembled *humans*.

The shadows started wrecking the place and the Secrecy stirred into chaos. The members with their powers tried to defeat the shadows, but whatever they threw at them seemed not to work. Tables flew from one end of the hall to the other while food flew everywhere.

"They're looking for something.." Destiny said while dodging a flying cup.

She was right. They rummaged through the stage and backstage until they focused on me. Their dark, soulless complexion was pointed towards me and Destiny.

"They're coming!" I yelled as they started speeding towards us.

Using my powers, I threw everything I had at them but it all just passed through them. Suddenly, an alarm started ringing through my ears and I realized what was happening. All hope was lost when suddenly, they looked above. Within a matter of seconds, all of the shadows suddenly disappeared as soon as they entered.

"You guys all ok?" Julius asked after coming towards me and Destiny.

"We're fine. But why did they leave that fast?" Destiny asked.

Then, Axel walked towards us and said, "Destiny, Austin, Julius, we need to discuss something. Follow me."

He wore a grave expression and his skin was pale. Something was wrong.

CHAPTER FIVE

A Stranger Appears

After the incident, Axel took us to the 5th floor. If you didn't know, the 5th floor was off-limits, but I had always wondered what it had in store for us and why no one was allowed.

As soon as I stepped out of the elevator, I was immediately confused: this was very different from the modern, and clean facility I had stayed in for the past 5 days. Dark blotches of dirt and whatnot covered some parts of the walls while the hum-buzz of the fluorescent lights flooded my ears. The confusing thing was that there was only one room on the whole floor. Axel took us in and I saw a marble pedestal standing in the middle of the room. It was meant to hold something important. The rest was just scrolls and books towering next to us like a library.

Julius scoured the place with awe in his eyes while Destiny flew upwards to check out the books. Axel wore the same expression which worried me. If he had to bring us here, the secret room on a secret floor, it must be serious.

"Let's cut to the chase," Axel said, grabbing everyone's attention.

"Tonight, when the shadows came, they came looking for something. It's called the Chrono Crystal, and brought by Sir Sebastian to the Secrecy, a name I'm sure you're familiar with."

Sir Sebastian, the man that created the Annihilator, the weapon we managed to find and hide away last year. The founder of the Secrecy.

"When Sebastian started the Secrecy, he always made sure the crystal and another weapon called the Annihilator, which I'm sure you're familiar with. He made sure these two weapons were hidden with extra caution. No one knows where he found it, but there's a legend from a long time ago."

Axel then brought out a scroll, presumably from this room itself. But this scroll was different. It had a deep red color and was written in white ink.

"The myth says that there's another other weapons from around that time." Axel said after unrolling the scroll. The scroll had a drawing of the Chrono Crystal, the Annihilator, and something else that was crossed out with gashes and rips,

"The last weapon's all ripped out...", Julius muttered under his breath.

"How is this related to powers going away?" Destiny asked.

"The Annihilator was a source of our powers along with the Chrono Crystal for the Secrecy. Although the comet gave us our powers originally, the Chrono Crystal helps to make our powers retain over our lives unlike the Annihilator which just amplifies powers when held. We usually store the crystal here, and our magicians have placed heavy protection over this area. Somehow, the shadows managed to bypass it and stole the crystal. Now everyone's power is lost completely. I can't shapeshift anymore. Julius will not be able to turn invisible. After the Chrono Crystal was stolen, everyone's powers are completely lost except...

"Except what?" Destiny said.

"Except *who*. You guys."

Silence flooded the room. Without the crystal, what is going to happen?

"What makes the situation worse is that we believe this won't be the last attack.

Suddenly, Axel's walkie-talkie spat out a few random panicking words.

"Hello? Guard? ... A trespasser?! I'm on my way." Axel said, speaking into the walkie-talkie.

"What was that?" Julius whispered to me.

"It sounds like someone just broke into the Secrecy." Destiny said.

"I have to go now. Stay here. Don't even think about leaving." Axel said sternly, as he walked out of the room and slammed the door shut.

"Well, I guess that means we follow him?" Destiny said.

"Let's go!" Julius said enthusiastically.

For the first time in a long time, I agreed with them because of the questions swimming in my head. Who is the trespasser? And what is the person going to do?

We snuck slowly and made our way to the first floor, making sure to keep a safe distance from Axel. Eventually, we followed him to the first elevator that led above the ground. I remembered how loud and rusty the elevator, but it seemed like the elevator was coing down. Axel paced around the entrance, waiting for it.

Finally the lift reached the floor. Light flickering, I could barely make out who was in the entrance.

"Who's that?" Julius yelled.

"Shut up!" Destiny said, but it was too late. Axel turned his attention towards us, but I saw something in the lift in front of him. Around five soldiers held down someone around the age of Julius with tattered clothes and pale skin. He looked like he had slept in a dumpster, but he had a strange, faint purple glow in his eyes.

"Wha- who are you? Why are you here?" Axel asked the kid, his voice filled with anger.

The kid responded calmy.

"A-Austin."

CHAPTER SIX

WE GET BRIEFED TO A DEATH MISSION

"Austin you know this kid?" asked Julius.

I analyzed his facial features, hair, clothing, and pretty much everything about him but I didn't recognize him one bit.

"Not really," I muttered.

Axel signaled the soldiers to take him somewhere else but in a panic, the person blurted out something, "The Chrono Crystal! I-I know where it is!"

Everyone paused. He knows where it is?

That could be the key to getting the crystal back and restoring the Secrecy's powers! I thought.

"What do you mean you know where it is?" Axel said.

"That's what you need right? The Chrono Crystal! The shadows stole it and are taking it somewhere. I'm here to help."

Axel studied the guy. His pale skin made him look like a ghost, and his ripped black hoodie and jeans added to his ghastly appearance.

"Guards, leave him. Follow me, kid."

The guards let him go and the guy ran towards us as soon as he was released. Axel brought him to the lounge, along with us three. The lounge was amazing, even at night when it was empty. A glistening chandelier lit up dozens of soft sofas and tables, while the night buffet was filled with pastries and snacks. Axel was still definitely mad at us for sneaking through, but I guess the trespasser more shook him up.

"What's your name?" Axel asked warmly, starting up the conversation.

"I-I don't know," he said.

"What do you mean you don't know?", asked Julius.

"I woke up a few days ago in some garage with a map and all my memory was lost. No matter how much I tried to remember stuff about me, I could only remember the name Austin."

Chills went down my spine as everyone looked at me.

"I already told you, I don't know who he is," I said.

"Then, I followed the map, got some supplies, and slept in the back of shops, until I reached here and got attacked by your guards." he continued. "You know the rest."

"I thought there was no map to the Secrecy, and we can only access it with the annoying crystal," Destiny asked Axel.

"You're right... How do you know where the Chrono Crystal is?" Axel replied.

"Well, technically I don't. But there was an incident not that long ago where some unexplainable shadows ravaged an airport. I saw it in a newspaper."

"Airport? Aren't we in a desert?" Destiny replied. She looked as confused as me.

"The nearest airport is around 3 hours away by car. And the incident happened an hour ago." Axel said, perplexed.

"Woah, they are really fast!" Julius exclaimed.

"The only reason they would go to an airport would be to hitch a ride," Axel said.

"Whatever it is, we need to leave soon if we want to make it." the mystery person said.

I thought about it thoroughly. Last time, we had Julius with his powers, the whole power of the Secrecy, and an ancient sword that amplified our powers by tenfold. Without any of that, the chances of getting the crystal back were slim. But something else bothered me. Why did the shadows need the crystal? And who were they?

"I can arrange a ride." Axel proposed.

I studied Destiny's expression. She was not one to back out from a challenge, so I wasn't that surprised at her reaction.

"Perfect! Let's go!" Destiny exclaimed and got out of her seat instantaneously.

"Wait up! What supplies do we get Axel?" Julius said.

"Come with me," Axel said.

Axel led us to another room on the ground floor and as soon as it opened, in the middle of the room with weapons and knives, there were *bracelets*.

"Wow, what a dangerous weapon. Bracelets." Julius said sarcastically.

"Try one then." Axel insisted.

Julius picked an icy-blue bracelet and as soon as he slipped it into in wrist, a miniature missile sped to one of the decoys in the weapons room, leaving a hole through it.

"Woah!" Julius exclaimed.

"They have different weapons, and they're much easier to carry than spears and machetes."

We all grabbed our weapons and gadgets. Destiny grabbed her bracelet and a watch which "did something cool" and she didn't want to tell me. and I grabbed a fiery red bracelet (which I was too scared to put on immediately so I was not sure what it did) and an umbrella (that I also had no idea what it did). The mystery dude didn't take any except his map, which worried me a little but if he survived days in the desert alone and found his way here, I had hope.

We said our goodbyes to Axel and the last thing he said was.

Be brave.

CHAPTER SEVEN

A Snake Wrecks an Airport

As soon as we left the Secrecy the only thing we could see looming far away was sand, sand, and sand.

I, Julius, Destiny, and the new dude sat in a luxurious limousine, keeping up with the Secrecy's "modern" standards, so I wasn't shocked. Hours passed as we got closer to the airport. To pass the time, we played games and got to know about the mystery person.

"Since you don't have a name and it's getting pretty tedious saying "new dude" every time, why don't you make one up?" I suggested.

After thinking for a while, he said "I'm not sure... nothing feels right. I wish I had my memory back."

"C'mon don't be so depressing. How about... Ghosty?" Julius asked, making me smack my forehead.

To my surprise, he said "I guess it's unique. Sure!"

With a new member of our little team, we continued on our journey until we finally reached our destination: the airport. This late in the night the airport was serene and calm, while waves of people and suitcases went past us and screens flashed in front of us.

"So how is this going to work?" Destiny said. Everyone stared at me, and the idea of being the leader was kind of uncomfortable. I racked my brain and thought about how we would find which plane the shadows went on, when they went, and where they went, and... well you get the idea.

"Well first we need to find out which plane the shadows got on.", I suggested

"I don't think that's going to be a problem," Ghosty said while pointing toward a sign, that read out "All flights to Cairo, Egypt are canceled." It was kind of eerie whenever Ghosty said anything, but whenever he said something it was valuable, so I was grateful.

"Egypt? Why are the shadows going there?" Destiny said out loud.

"Maybe their master is there? Whatever it is we need to get there somehow. Any ideas?" Julius asked.

"Let's just go to a Help Desk," Ghosty said while he zoomed toward one.

We all ran towards the desk and asked the official about any flights going to Egypt. While she said there weren't any flights things took a turn for the worst as I felt a hand on my shoulder. In a panic, I spun around and saw a man dressed in a black jacket and sunglasses, like the leader of a gang. He wore a crooked smile brimming with gold teeth and a few others like him stood behind him.

"The Hazard 6!" Destiny yelled with awe in her eyes. I rolled my eyes to the back of my head. When we were living "normal" lives, Destiny used to love a rock band called the Hazard 6, and she was obsessed! What were the chances that we met them today?!

"Hey gang, y'all want me to sign something?" the leader of the group said in a Southern accent. "We're going on tour to Egypt! Never been there before, but should be a rockin' show."

"Wait aren't all the flights to Egypt cancelled?" Julius asked curiously, and I was pretty sure he also had never heard of the band.

"Yup, apparently something wrong happened with a cargo plane to Egpyt, so there's a delay for all the normal flights. But, we have a private jet that's flying there." another member of the group answered.

Ghosty shot me a look and I immediately understood what he meant. We HAD to sneak onto the plane if we wanted any chance of getting the crystal back. Ghosty immediately started asking questions to get more information.

"When's your flight leaving?" Ghosty asked them, trying not to sound creepy.

While signing Destiny's cap, the leader, whose name we later found out was Chuck, said "In around 15 minutes, we're getting late so I'll see y'all later!"

As the Hazard 6 left (Destiny was miserable), we all knew what we had to do next.

We had to sneak onto that plane.

I had never known about the process of getting on a private jet, but as soon as I saw how Hazard 6 could get on their flight in minutes, I immediately knew I had to get a private plane when I got a job. But for now, time was ticking and we needed to find a way onto the flight. After talking for a bit, and analyzing the security in the airport, we all knew there was no way we could get through normally.

But we were kids with superpowers, so the normal way was out of the picture.

"We could sneak our way to the plane," Julius suggested.

"I don't think we could get through all the security like that," I replied.

"Well, then I guess we'll have to force our way through," Ghosty said.

Everyone accepted it and with around 10 minutes left until the private jet would go, we immediately got to work. However, as we sped towards the security section of the airport, I noticed something in the corner of my eye. Well not really something, more like someone. 3 people in dark clothing with a strange symbol on their forehead stared in our direction, and I could tell they meant trouble. With a glint in their eyes, I noticed something in one of their pockets. Not a weapon or an explosive, but a purple sphere. Before I could tell what had happened, I heard screams behind me and then I saw it: a shadow must be larger than the other ones, but it was in the shape of a snake, with colossal fangs, but with glowing eyes that stared through my skull.

Although the airport was in chaos and we could have easily made it to the flight, we needed to protect everyone in the airport from this shadow-snake thing. Julius and Ghosty quickly read my expression and got to work, bringing out their weapons and trying to distract the snake from the airport. Just like the shadows, whatever was sent at the thing went through the thing. However, as I scanned the area, I noticed the 3 people in dark clothing escaping the airport, and I knew I had to act quickly.

I ran towards the snake, throwing everything near me telekinetically towards him, but it wasn't effective, and he continued sweeping through everything. In the fury of luggage and bags, Destiny had flown back to me, and in her hands were 3 purple spheres. She had defeated the men, stolen the spheres, and returned all by herself. Sometimes I forgot how powerful she was, but there was no time to admire that. I examined the sphere, but the glow faded quickly, and suddenly it didn't have that feel that I usually felt with magical items.

On the other side, Julius and Ghosty started moving people out of the area but signaled to us that the band was leaving in around 3 minutes. The situation was looking grim; the snake looked at me with a cynical smirk, and nothing we threw at it worked at all. I started to think about the earlier incident at the party, but the shadows just left on their own in that incident, so it was of no use. I looked at my weapons, but they were all out of reach.

But then I stared at Ghosty, and I realized the snake didn't even see him. Destiny and I ran towards him, and amazingly, Ghosty was our shield as the snake went towards the rest of the civilians. Suddenly, the snake fizzed out in a spectacular display of purple and darkness, and the mist that the snake transformed into drifted toward the purple ball, like a storage device. Destiny's eyelids opened wide, as the purple ball glowed like normal just like the other two.

The strange thing was that Ghosty didn't even look fazed, and it looked like this was his 9-5 job. I remember when I first got introduced to this strange world, and I felt like a fish out of water. But I had a deep feeling about Ghosty, that something more dark was behind his memory wipe. The 3 purple balls sat squarely in my hands as I realized those men who had them could summon these shadow monsters at will. That was when I realized how dire the situation was that we were about to get into. As I pondered my thoughts, Julius knocked on my head.

"Hey! The flight is delayed for around half an hour because of the whole massive snake situation. Let's go explore!" He said with a gleam in his eyes. Destiny and Ghosty also stood behind him and I had no choice but to go with him. But that uneasy feeling I had about Ghosty lingered with me through the whole little journey, but in the end, I decided to think about that on the flight. Speaking of the flight, we had to find a way to sneak onto it without rousing any suspicion.

"Any ideas?" I asked everyone.

We thought about it for a few minutes, rummaging through our bags and looking around the airport for a solution. The flight was minutes away from departing so we had to make it quick. With a cookie that I got from the airport stuffed in my mouth, I finally uncovered something.

An umbrella that I brought from the gadget room. I still had no idea what it did, but I opened it to check it out. Suddenly, a forcefield-like veil covered me and my stomach churned with nausea. What just happened? However, judging from everyone else's expression, nothing had really happened. Welp, it would have been really cool if I turned invisible there, I thought to myself.

Suddenly, Destiny yelled, "Austin, w-what in the world is happening to you!".

Then, I stared at my clothes, and I was stunned! I wore a beach T-shirt with blue shorts with a shark pattern on them: the same as the leader of the Hazard 6, Chuck, wore! My legs extended like slime as my nose elongated and my hair grew into a long mullet. It was amazing, and just what we needed to get on the plane: I had transformed into him! I handed the umbrella to the rest of the group, and they amazingly turned into other band members. It felt so weird looking at my friends suddenly turn into a group of adults with beards and earrings, but we had little time left to get onto the plane. However, our whole ride rode on the fact that we would be let in without any identification.

We made our way to the plane, with mixed feelings. As soon as we got there, the myriad of securty guards gave suspicious looks, and I knew there was no way they'd let us in. However, miraculously, we were let into the private jet! As we climbed up the staircase to the plane, a wave of relief washed over me: We were going to Egpyt! The private jet was the stuff of dreams! The seats were as cushiony as clouds, and we had enough legroom to do jumping jacks. We took off almost immediately, and through one of the windows, I could see the real Hazard 6 down below, probably really confused as to why the plane had taken off without them. With Destiny behind me humming music, and Julius playing with his phone, we sat on the plane and stared off into the distance.

CHAPTER EIGHT

RIDE ON A PRIVATE JET

The plane ride was smooth and luxurious! I mean, other than our disguises wearing out twice during the flight, the private jet was the amazing! We all had our personal bar - I was crazed at first, but then I remembered we were impersonating adults. Other than that, waitresses came and went, answering our every need and making me feel like royalty.

I stared outside the plane into the cloudy night sky. We'd been on such a journey and still hadn't reached the hardest part: getting the crystal back. I still had no idea how we were going to rescue the crystal, let alone how we were even going to find where the shadows went.

As if all of this wasn't enough, the feeling that there was something more to Ghosty's memory wipe nagged me. Why didn't the shadow-snake go after Ghosty? It was like he was never there. And he didn't look fazed at all, even though he was recently introduced to this confusing and terrifying world of magical powers! It was almost like... he was familiar with this somehow.

Before I could finish my thoughts, Destiny yelled my name to start talking about the plan and what we were going to do after we land.

"Alright so what are we going to do once we land?" Julius asked.

"Reminder that we still look like 40 year old rockstars" Destiny added.

"Well I guess we find out where in the world the shadows went?" Ghosty suggested.

"There's no pattern to their movements..." I muttered.

"But one thing stays the same." Ghosty said.

"What?"

"They always make headlines on the news" Ghosty replied. "We can easily find out where they're going with that."

It hadn't crossed my mind that the normal world had been keeping track of the shadows for us. I wondered what the normal world would think was happening, but the truth was we were as confused as they were. We were against an enemy we couldn't touch, and although we had managed to defeat Orion, it still dawned on me how hard this mission was going to be.

"Well I guess that's how we'll find them. When we land, we'll call Axel and check out the situation of the shadows. We'll follow them and try to retrieve the crystal and head back to HQ with it. Everyone alright with the plan?" I asked.

"Yup" Julius said. "How are we going to defeat the shadows anyways though? Anything we throw at them just goes through them anyways."

"We'll figure it out"

A few hours passed by, and the jet began its descent into the glow of the Dubai skyline, the desert stretching endlessly. The conversation had wound down, and everyone seemed lost in their thoughts. Destiny sat cross-legged, flipping through a map of recent shadow sightings on her tablet. Julius leaned back in his seat, arms crossed, seemingly asleep, but I knew he was awake, thinking, as usual. Ghosty, however, was staring out the window, his reflection looking eerily blank in the glass.

As the plane touched down and we disembarked in our disguises, Ghosty hesitated momentarily on the stairs, his gaze fixating on the carpet of the private jet's stairs. I slowed my pace to walk beside him.

"You good?" I asked.

"Yeah," Ghosty replied quickly, but something about his voice didn't sit right. It was like he wasn't entirely sure. I wanted to press him further but decided just to let it be. Although I couldn't really shake off my suspicions of Ghosty, we had enough on our plate without adding Ghosty's cryptic mood.

"Let's go. We've got a crystal to find."

I had never really understood the concept of fame and riches, but I guess disgiusing as world famous rockstars gives you a pretty profound idea. Soon after landing and getting into a jet-black limousine with way too many bodyguards for just 4 people, we made our way to a hotel. I had never been to Dubai, but it was a breathtaking place, however the heat of the desert made it feel like I was sitting in a moving microwave.

While Julius flapped a newspaper to get rid of the heat, my phone rang. Fumbling through my bag, I grabbed my vibrating phone and Axel was calling. I picked up the phone and pressed it to my ear.

"Hi Axel, we just landed in Dubai. Sorry for not calling we were a bit busy."

"That's great Austin, things aren't going that well here."

"What do you mean?" I asked, concerned.

"A majority of the Secrecy is panicked. I mean they've lived their whole lives with their powers. There are some reports that some members are going to stage a riot, so I hope it's going well over there." he said. "Any altercations with the shadows yet?"

I paused. Axel was already in enough pressure with the whole Secrecy in hysteria, he didn't need any more stress.

"No, it's been smooth sailing over here."

"Are you sure Austin?" he said, questioning the anxiety in my voice.

"Yup!" I said energetically, hoping he bought my lie.

After somehow believing my lie, I told him about everything that happened (leaving out the shadow snake incident).

"Well, I do have a few connections near the hotel you guys are staying at. You should get ready to move as soon as you reach the hotel. The shadows don't reach in a few hours due to a delay, so every second we gain on them counts."

"Where are we headed?" Julius asked as he could hear the conversation because he was next to me.

"Cairo, Egpyt," Axel said.

CHAPTER NINE

Take to the Skies

We reached the hotel, and after checking in and settling into our rooms, we met back in my room to discuss the plan. The hotel was amazing, with sky-high chandeliers, silky smooth beds, and a breathtaking skyline view. However, the pressing matter was that the flight the shadows were on wouldn't be delayed forever, and we could never reach them in time, even with the fastest car. That's when Axel suggested something.

"I have connections with a friend not too far from your hotel. He has a small airplane and enough resources that should be enough for you to get to Cairo fast enough to intercept the shadows." Axel said.

"That's great!" Destiny said with relief.

"His name is Khalid and he's a retired pilot, I trust him with my life so there's nothing to worry about. He'll be there to pick you guys up in 20 minutes, so get ready."

"Thanks, Axel," I said.

"We're all counting on you guys," Axel said, before hanging up the call.

We made our way to the hotel lobby, and it was quieter than I expected. The usual bustle of a luxury hotel was gone, making it feel as if we were in a library. We gathered in the corner of the lobby, with a small restaurant, and cushioned seats everywhere. Ghosty was staring off into the distance again, making me feel as if he was reluctant to go ahead with the plan, but we all were nervous about the mission, so I could understand. Julius was playing with a coaster, and wolfing down an untouched plate of muffins on the table.

"He's late." Destiny muttered half an hour later.

"Give him some time, he'll be here soon," I replied.

A few minutes later, just as I was texting Axel, a man approached our table. It looked like he was in his 50s, with weathered skin and a neat beard and sharp eyes. He wore a leather jacket and had a warm smile.

"You must be the band Axel told me about. My name's Khalid, heard you guys are in need of a ride", the man said in a deep voice. His gaze wavered over all of us, staying on Ghosty a beat longer than the rest.

"Nice to meet you," I said, standing up to shake his hand.

"Mind if I join?", Khalid said, motioning to the seat opposite to us.

"By all means," Julius said, gesturing dramatically as if he was talking to royalty.

Ignoring the sarcasm, Khalid said, "Axel told me a little bit about your situation. Says you guys need help getting to Cairo. Says you guys need help catching someone?"

"You could say that," Destiny said.

"We can talk on the way to the airstrip, follow me.", Khalid said, standing up.

We all followed him to the hotel exit, got in a spacious, brown jeep, and made our way to the airstrip.

"Cairo airspace is crawling with security and patrol, especially after what happened in the airport in California. We'll need to avoid that and pass through without suspicions. It's not exactly easy, and not cheap either." Khalid said, while on the wheel.

"We can pay," I said.

"With what?" Khalid said while laughing. "You guys look like you've spent your last pennies on room service."

"Axel can take care of the money part. Just focus on helping us get to Cairo."

"Alright boss," he said. "Axel saved my skin more than once, so consider the favour repaid. Anyways, we're already here."

The airstrip looked eerily dark and quiet, but it wasn't surprising considering it was almost midnight. The full moon illuminated the sky. Large lights blinded me as everyone exited the vehicle.

"I'm pretty sure this is how horror movies start," Julius said after hearing a cracking noise.

"We'll be fine," Destiny said while rolling her eyes. "How much time will it take to get to Cairo anyways?"

"Around 5 hours at best." Khalid answered. "It should be just in time to intercept the shadows at the airport."

As we passed through security, we eventually reached the airstrip, which stretched endlessly past my view. On the airstrip was a sleek, white aircraft.

"Looks great!" Ghosty said

We piled our few belongings into the plane while Khalid went through his pre-flight checks. As I watched him work, I couldn't help but feel the weight of what was ahead. The shadows weren't going to wait for us to catch up, and every second felt like we were losing ground.

"Everyone buckled in?" Khalid called out, climbing into the cockpit.

I glanced around. Julius was already leaning back, arms crossed like he wasn't worried at all. Destiny sat near a window, her fingers drumming anxiously on the armrest. Ghosty was at the back, staring out the small side window again, his face unreadable.

"Ready," I said.

Khalid started the engines, and the plane roared to life. As we taxied to the runway, I tried to push away the gnawing doubts in my mind. How we were going to get there in time. How the shadows seemed to ignore him.

I didn't know what we'd find in Cairo, but one thing was certain—we were flying straight into the unknown.

CHAPTER TEN

BLUEPRINTS OF CHAOS

The next few hours were insignificant: Destiny took a nap, I played card games with Julius, and Ghosty insisted on being in the cockpit, which only confused me more.

Suddenly, Khalid said, "Guys there's something up. Get over here."

We rushed to the cockpit to see everything seemingly fine and Ghosty sitting calmly with Khalid.

"There's a new update on the flight time," Khalid said, stressed.

"I knew we'd get there late," Julius muttered.

"It's not about being late," Khalid said, overhearing. "It's quite the opposite. We will reach Cairo Airport slightly earlier than as the shadows' plane.

I puffed a sigh of relief.

"That's perfect! We'll have enough time to intercept the shadows in the airport, and everything should go smoothly." Julius exclaimed.

"About that... Khalid and I have been talking, and we've come up with an alternate plan to approach the shadows. Instead of trying to get the payload on the ground, we could directly grab it from the plane's cargo. That way it would be an unexpected apprehension, and they would not expect it at all."

I was confused on why he said payload, but then I remembered Khalid still had no idea why we were doing this whole mission.

"Wouldn't that be unsafe for the pilots?" Julius asked.

"If Austin will be able to close the door at the end with his powers, nothing will be noticed except a few missing cargo." Khalid said.

"I still don't think it's a good idea... we can just wait for them to land and get the crystal back on the ground." Destiny said.

"We already know how hard it is to deal with the shadows, let alone when they'll be expecting an attack. Apprehending them midair might be our best shot. What do you think Austin?" Ghosty said.

I thought for a bit, and then said, "We'll be right back Khalid.", and then exited the cockpit with the rest.

"Okay, okay," I answered, rubbing my temple. "Let's break this down logically. What do we know?"

Destiny leaned in. "One: They don't know we're coming. Two: They have to be transporting the crystal somehow. It's not like a shadow can just hold an object that important just like that."

I nodded slowly. "Which means there's a container. Maybe something physical we can grab."

Julius exhaled, "And what about them? We still can't fight shadows like normal enemies."

"We don't need to," I said. The idea was forming in my head, risky but possible. "We just need to get in, grab the crystal, and get out before they can react."

Ghosty tilted his head. "And how do you suggest we get in?"

Silence.

Then, Destiny smirked. "Midair boarding."

Julius let out a short laugh. "You're insane."

"Am I?" Destiny shot back. "I can fly, Julius. I can carry one of you over if we get close enough. And if Logan can match speed with the other plane for even a few minutes, it could work."

"*If* you can get in the plane first wihout getting sucked into the atmosphere."

Ghosty muttered under his breath, shaking his head. "This is the dumbest plan I've ever heard."

"Got a better one?" Destiny challenged.

"Actually, yes. We can just wait until they land and we can get the crystal normally like we planned!" Ghosty retorted.

I took a deep breath, my pulse already quickening at the sheer insanity of what we were considering. "Alright. If we do this, we need a strategy. Destiny and I will get onto the plane first."

Julius sighed. "I'll go invisible and slip in behind you."

"I thought your powers don't work."

"I'll be close enough to the crystal to get my powers back temporarily." Julius replied.

Ghosty added, "And I'll stay here with Khalid."

"We're really doing this," I murmured.

Destiny grinned. "Oh, we so are."

CHAPTER ELEVEN

CRATES RUIN A MID-AIR HEIST

Eventually, we saw a hint of white travelling fast through the night sky. Khalid travelled closer to it and soon it was obvious, a massive cargo plane, definitely the one that the shadows had taken.

"Alright guys, the plane will reach the airport in around 10 minutes, so this operation has to be finished in less than 7 minutes if you guys want to avoid any attention." Khalid said.

"Are you sure that's the plane?" I asked to confirm.

"I'm certain." He replied, and a wave of panic washed over me. What would happen if something went wrong?

Once we got close enough to the plane, we equipped Destiny with a walkie-talkie to communicate. A few minutes passed and we were just close enough that Destiny wouldn't have much problem flying, and the pilots wouldn't notice our plane. We were finally ready for the operation. Ghosty's hands twitched, looking a little uncertain about the whole operation, but I told myself I would tell Destiny and Julius my suspicions about him after we got the crystal back.

After testing the walkie talkies and reviewing the plan, it was finally time to carry out the mission. Everything was ready in place, and the whole Secrecy depended on us.

"Ready?" Destiny said, ready to jump off the plane.

"Ready, go for it." Khalid replied, setting his 7 minute timer and starting it.

Destiny, and Julius who was equipped with a automatically deploying parachute, jumped off the plane door, and suddenly disappeared from my view, making me panic for a second, until they reappeared. The wind at that altitude definitely was a big challenge, but Destiny managed to fly and steer Julius with her in the right direction.

"Khalid let's go to the plane." I suggested.

"Alright, you should probably hold on to something though," Khalid said before zooming ahead towards the plane, making me and Ghosty stumble.

Destiny and Julius were standing on the wing of the plane, and I got close enough to open the door of the cargo plane. Well, open is kind of a lie. After focusing all my energy on the cargo plane, the door flew away and zoomed past us, along with a few crates.

"Austin what are you doing!" Destiny yelled through the walkie.'

"It's not my fault the door was weak! Go we don't have enough time!"

Suddenly, a purple aura started covering Julius, and for the first time in a long time, I saw him turn invisible. I wonder how it would've felt to get your powers back after so long. As the cargo plane zoomed by, we quickly flew away from the plane, and I turned to the camera we attached to Destiny.

"You guys see the crystal yet?" I asked Destiny through the walkie.

"No not yet, they must've hidden it pretty well. Also it feels pretty strange though. I thought we'd face some kind of resistance from the shadows." She replied.

The inside of the cargo plane was dark, filled to the brim with crates painted with fragile and careful stickers. I switched over to Julius' camera view, and although he was shovelling through crate after crate, he still couldn't find anything that looked like it had a crystal.

Destiny and Julius moved through the cramped plane, sifting through crate after crate, frustration growing.

"Still nothing," he muttered through the walkie. "If the crystal's here, it's not out in the open."

Destiny frowned. "Then that means it's secured somewhere. Maybe in a hidden compartment or—"

A eerie, unnatural hiss boomed through my walkie-talkie.

Destiny and Julius suddenly froze.

"Did you hear that?" Destiny whispered.

The walkie crackled in my ear. "Guys, something's moving in there," I said, trying to keep my voice steady. "Be careful."

A sudden thud made Destiny spin around. One of the larger crates shifted slightly at the back of the plane.

Julius barely had time to react before the crate exploded outward, splintering into shards of wood. An army of shadows surged forward, combining forming into a humanoid figure with glowing violet eyes.

"Destiny, get out of there!" I yelled.

But before she could react, the shadow lunged fast.

Destiny dodged just in time, the shadow's clawed hand slicing through the air where she'd just been. Julius, still invisible, used the opportunity to slip behind it. He grabbed a crowbar from the floor and swung—only for it to pass straight through the shadow like mist.

"Great," he muttered. "Forgot about that."

Another hiss echoed through the cargo hold.

"Oh, come on," Destiny groaned.

One by one, the crates burst open, revealing more shadow creatures, their eyes locking onto Destiny and Julius like predators spotting their prey.

"This was a trap," I realized, my stomach twisting. "They wanted us to come here."

Ghosty, watching the live feed beside me, exhaled sharply. "We need to get them out of there. Now."

But Destiny wasn't backing down.

"We're not leaving without that crystal."

Julius dodged another swipe, rolling into the shadows. "Sure, but it'd be great if we had a way to actually hurt these things."

Suddenly, at the edge of the camera view, there was a metal briefcase. It was small, barely noticeable among the crates, but it gave off a faint glow—the same glow I'd seen in the Chrono Crystal before.

"The briefcase to your left," I whispered. "Looks like thats it."

Destiny bolted toward the case, but the shadows moved to intercept.

"Julius, cover me!"

"With what? Harsh language?"

"Just do something!"

"Julius the times ticking!" Khalid said through the walkie.

I stared at the timer. There was 30 seconds left until the plane was going to taxi.

"You guys have half a minute!" Ghosty shouted.

"Julius try to lose their attention and turn invisible!" I said through the walkie.

"On it!"

Julius ran past a few shadows, and turned invisible without any shadow noticing. Everyone stayed silent on the walkie-talkie as his camera went closer and closer to the metal briefcase. After slowly moving a crate to the side, he unbuckled the suitcase, and there it was: the Chrono Crystal shined brightly, illuminating the cargo hold. However, just as Julius was about to pick it up, something unimaginable happened.

"Austin it's not the crystal!" Julius said, confused.

"Huh?" I said, and then I saw his hand pass through the crystal, making the crystal shimmer.

It was a *hologram.*

"Oh my god..." Ghosty gasped.

A new voice crackled into our earpieces. Cold.

"You think you've won?"

My blood turned to ice.

"Ah Austin, I knew you were desperate for the crystal but performing a mid-air heist was beyond crazy."

"Destiny! Julius! Get out of there!" I shouted, ignoring the voice.

"Don't need to tell me twice!" Destiny's voice crackled through the walkie talkie.

"You took the bait." the voice amused. "We'll meet again." the voice said, before disappearing.

Just as the cargo plane landed on the ground, Destiny and Julius flew away, back to our jet. We had failed to get the crystal, and the shadows knew we were going to be there the whole time. But the question racked my mind. How did they predict that we were going to intercept them

mid-air. They could've guessed perfectly somehow or...
There was well-placed mole.

CHAPTER TWELVE

COFFEE OF FAILURE

"So, what do we do now?" I said, while sitting in a café with Julius, Ghosty, and Destiny. We had to say farewell to Khalid after the mission failed, but before he left he gave us the location of a nice café in Cairo, so we decided to stop by.

As my fingers traced the rim of my coffee cup absentmindedly, my mind kept on replaying the failed heist like a broken recorder. I glanced at Julius, Ghosty, and Destiny, all of us still processing what had happened in the air.

"I told Axel about the mid-air interception, and he thinks it's quite dangerous to further go for the crystal anyways."

Julius took a slow sip from his own cup, eyes distant. "Axel's right. We shouldn't rush in without a plan. Last time, we barely made it out. A hologram, really?"

Ghosty let out a frustrated sigh, leaning back in his chair. "Doesn't change the fact that the shadows are getting closer. The Chrono Crystal is right there in their hands. We can't just sit here and do nothing."

Suddenly, screams filled our ears, coming from a screen in the shop.

"What's that?" Destiny said.

A news reporter talked about a massive sandstorm near the pyramids of Giza.

"Wait that might be the shadows."

Destiny tapped the table, her gaze sharp. "We have to get to the pyramids before they do. The Eclipse leader won't wait around forever. We know they're after the crystal, and we're the only ones who can stop them."

I looked at them, anxiety settling in my voice. "But Axel said it's too dangerous. If we go, we might not come back."

Julius leaned forward, his voice low but firm. "If we don't go, they win. We've been fighting for this crystal for too long to turn back now. Let's go for it."

"And what's the point of being part of the Secrecy if we don't stop them? We've come too far to back out now." Destiny said, smiling. The news anchor on the screen shifted to a new segment.

> *"...Authorities have confirmed unusual activity near the Giza pyramids. Several reports of strange figures and sudden shifts in the environment, possibly related to recent sightings of the so-called shadow-creatures—"*

I glanced at the others. We didn't need to hear more. "Alright," I said, standing up, a sudden surge of adrenaline pushing through me. "We go to the pyramids, confront the leader of the shadows, and get the Chrono Crystal back. Axel's not gonna like it, but we don't have a choice."

We caught an Uber to the pyramids, our minds set on getting the crystal back, but we decided to not tell Axel until we actually had it in our hands. The ride was long, but the situation made the time seem to drag on forever.

I still hadn't told Destiny and Julius about my suspicions of Ghosty being a mole, and ratting away our location to the shadows. I had a gnawing feeling that he was faking his memory loss, and he definitely was part of the shadows.

Eventually, we reached the pyramids, and the sight of them was nothing short of breathtaking. The towering structures loomed in the distance, their stone faces glinting in the setting sun. The desert stretched out in all directions, vast and unending. The silence was almost surreal, broken only by the soft hum of the car's engine as it slowed to a stop.

Hordes of tourists flew by us as we went closer to the pyramids. In the corner of my eye, I could make out an area covered with yellow police tape.

Julius, as usual, was the first to speak. "I still don't like this. The Eclipse could be anywhere around here."

Ghosty nodded, his expression unreadable. "It feels weird."

A tourist approached us, holding a few pairs of uncanny glasses.

"Eclipse." I could make out of his thick accent.

I looked at the sun, and I saw the sun covered partially by a black circle.

"Oh, a solar eclipse. We'll take a few of those."

After paying for the glasses, we ventured further. Destiny was already scanning the surroundings, her eyes sharp. "We can't waste time. We need to get inside before they trap us. Let's just head to the area with police tape."

I felt my heart race as I took a deep breath, trying to focus. "Right. Stay alert, and be careful. The last thing we need is to walk right into a trap like last time."

We started walking toward the base of the pyramids, our steps slow but purposeful. The shadows of the ancient structures stretched long across the sand, and the air seemed to grow heavier with every step. Something about the place felt off, like the desert air was holding it's breath in anticipation.

Suddenly, a voice echoed through the air, startling us all. "I knew you'd come," it said, low and menacing. I recognized the voice

We froze, looking around. "Show yourself!" Destiny called.

The sand beneath us started swirling, and we all fell down into darkness.

CHAPTER THIRTEEN

GHOSTY MAKES A CHOICE

After falling for a second or two, we landed on a hard, marble floor that sent shivers down my spine. There was no light except for one lit candle about to melt away

"You should have stayed away," the Eclipse leader said, their voice dripping with disdain. "Now you'll learn why you were never meant to possess the Chrono Crystal."

I recognized his voice, and I realized that he was the one that intercepted our radio channel during the heist. The whole area looked massive, as if they had a whole society right under the pyramids.

"Where's our crystal!" Julius shouted to the hooded leader.

"Your crystal?" The leader said, laughing, his laugh reverberating around the dark hall we landed him.

"Yeah our crystal! If you didn't know, your shadow people went halfway across the world to steal our crystal." Destiny said.

"Is that what they told you guys? That it was your crystal?" he said. The leader unveiled his cloak, revealling the shining Chrono Crystal.

"This was never yours to begin with. The Secrecy had stolen the crystal from The Eclipse 500 years ago."

"The Eclipse?" I asked. "What's that?"

"It's the name of our society, but that's not what's important. What's important is how we suffered for 500 years, powerless without the crystal. But we adapted. We prevailed. We learned how to transform into a forbidden form created by the first powered people themselves: the shadow form." he said, while staring at Ghosty.

Suddenly, a wind started swirling around Ghosty, and he turned into a shadow.

"What's happening?" Ghosty said himself, but I was buying none of it.

"I knew you were faking everything! You were part of the Eclipse the whole time!" I yelled with rage at Ghosty.

"Oh, it was all planned. Every single thing was planned. We sent that shadow to the Secrecy base just to guide you guys here. Of course, we had to wipe him of his memory for a while, but by now it must've come back." the leader said right before snapping, the sound reverberating around the hall.

Ghosty reverted back to a human, his blank expression he always wore replaced with a complexion that was filled with sympathy and guilt.

"I- I'm sorry, I had no idea." Ghosty said with his head down, still head pointing down.

I glanced at the crystal in the leader's hand.

Destiny stepped forward, fists clenched. "You were one of them this whole time?"

Ghosty's voice was barely above a whisper. "I swear, I didn't know. I didn't remember anything until just now." His hands were shaking, but there was no time to argue with Ghosty about his loyalty.

The Eclipse leader smirked. "It doesn't matter. What matters is that the crystal is back where it belongs." He lifted it slightly, the golden glow of the Chrono Crystal reflecting in his eyes. "And with it, we will ensure that the Secrecy is never able to suppress us again."

I gritted my teeth. I didn't care about their history. I didn't care about their reasons. All I knew was that we couldn't let them keep the crystal.

Suddenly, I felt a wave pass through me, almost just like the feeling of adrenaline I got when I first got my powers. Except it was reversed, as if the feeling was being sucked out of me.

"What's happening?" Julius said after fluctuating between invisible and visible.

"That's the total eclipse. It's the first total eclipse in hundreds of years visible from Egypt. It's been known to emasculate the strength of your powers. The only reason your powers are still working is you are right next to the crystal. However, us shadows don't get weakened by the eclipse. We get amplified. Strengthened."

"Hence the name of your society." Destiny said.

Julius leaned toward me and whispered, "You have a plan?"

"Working on it." I muttered.

"Ghosty, you said you lead us over here because your memory was partly wiped right?" I said, while trying to wear a sly smirk on my face to throw off the Eclipse Leader.

"Yeah, I would neve-" Ghosty started, but I interrupted him.

"Prove it. Take the crystal." I challenged.

"Don't be stupid," the leader said, with anger growing in his voice. His gaze shifted to Ghosty. "You've been in the Eclipse since you were a kid, haven't you Max? Are you really going to sacrifice it all for some friends you have met for a day?"

Your real name was Max? I thought in my head. "Your last chance to choose. Max, don't do this."

He wore a

"I'm sorry," he said before lunging.

CHAPTER FOURTEEN

WE DEMOLISH THE PYRAMIDS

Suddenly, Ghosty transformed into a shadow and lunged towards... us. Not the leader, Vesper, who had taken away his memory and talked to him like he was an experimental rat, us. His friends.

He slammed into me with full force, more powerful than any shadow that we'd encountered. But it's not the impact that hurt me, it's the choice. Ghosty's, or whatever his name was, choice. However, I had no time to think about that, and instead I wrestled Ghosty away, and ran towards Vesper, who was already walking away.

Just as I was about to catch up with Destiny and Julius, who were both already tailing Vesper, a myriad of shadows lunged at us again. It looked as if hope was lost, as we drowned in the icy grasp of the shadows.

"I got this." Julius said, struggling under the grasp of the shadows. We were all knocked down to the floor by the impact, but I managed to strangle my way free. I tried to lift an object from my backpack with my powers, but my powers were sucked dry due to the total eclipse. I ran towards Vesper, who was calmy walking away, as if nothing was happening. Right before I started to chase him, I stared back. Destiny and Julius were fighting off the shadows, and it didn't look that great for them. However, the crystal was our first priority, so I told myself I'd come back to them right after I grabbed the crystal

"I'll be right back." I muttered, and accelerated towards the leader, when suddenly a door dropped down from behind me, and the candles supplying light went out. I stayed calm however, and tried to find Vesper in the pitch black darkness.

Suddenly, light filled the room, and Vesper was standing next to a weapon: a long scepter, adorned with a few purple crystals, and topped with a crescent.

"Looks like you've never seen this before. Well that's because the Secrecy hid it from you. The Shadow Scepter, the last weapon of the Big 3, along with the Annihilator, and the crystal I have in my hand." He said with a sly smirk.

After tapping the scepter on the ground, suddenly Vesper transformed into a shadow much more grand than anything we'd ever seen before, a massive shadow creature with glowing blue eyes, overflowing with pure power.

I scanned my surroundings, for cover, weapons, anything! But the room was barren. However, I suddenly remembered something I had around my wrist: my bracelet weapon. I was still unsure if it would even work, considering it could only be activated by powered people, and with my powers barely working, I doubted I would even be considered powered.

"Austin, I respect you for your never faltering persistence. But you should've turned back since your mid-air heist," He said, making me remember that failure we had. It couldn't happen again. It wouldn't happen again.

He levelled his scepter up to my head. "Although I would love to set you free, unfortunately we don't free witnesses, and that's how our society has stayed hidden for so long. Austin, we would value your powers, along with your twin and friend. I propose that you join the Eclipse."

I stumbled. Join the Eclipse? The unknown rival society of the Secrecy? The thought ran through my head for a bit. I mean the story that Vesper said earlier about the crystal rightfully being theirs started to not seem that crazy after all.

"No. No way I'd join your wretched society. Not even if the world ended." I spat. Although I considered it for a second, there was no way I'd betray the whole Secrecy just like that.

"Then it's settled," he said, as he channeled his energy through the scepter, which was pointing to my kneeling body. Shivers ran my down my spine, and my brain screamed *"This is the end!"*. I raised my hand for impact, my heart beating out of my chest, and then I heard a boom.

When I opened my eyes, I saw 20 people who looked exactly like me. I'd always wondered what would happen when I die, but I didn't know this was it. My heart raced as I scanned my surroundings, and it was at that moment when I saw Vesper, circling around attacking every version of me. And that was when I realized what had happened: the energy beam from his scepter had hit my bracelet, and I guess the power of my bracelet was to make copies of my self, which was quite a neat power.

With my newfound discovery of what my bracelet did, I lunged over to Vesper and fumbled through the pockets of his cloak, that had dropped on the floor after his transformation. My hands trembled as I heard boom after boom, shaking the entire room. Suddenly, I felt something smooth, and I pulled it out. It was the Chrono Crystal in all it's might, and definitely not a hologram. It's glow illuminated the room, and rejuvenated me with strength. There was no time to lose however, as Vesper raised his sceptre towards the real me, but luckily I dodged it with perfect accuracy, making the energy beam break open the door instead.

With adrenaline fueling me, I leaped through the door, jagged metal cutting my arms, and ran to around where we fell from. Destiny and Julius were fighting a shadow bigger than the rest, which I assumed to be Ghosty. Destiny's eyes widened as she saw the crystal in my hand, and Julius leaped with pain as he took a hard blow from Ghosty.

"You got it! Let's get out of here!" Destiny yelled.

Behind me, I could hear louder and louder energy blasts as Vesper had a enraged look in his eyes, burning with fury.

"YOU WON'T GET AWAY WITH THIS!" He shouted, making me tremble a bit.

"I have an idea." Destiny said, before flying over to Vesper (albeit really slowly due to the eclipse) and redirecting the scepter's aim towards the hole we fell through, which was now covered.

"What are you doin- NO!" Vesper said as a energy blast travelled above my head, singeing a few hairs, and blasting open a hole.

Suddenly, I felt a wave of adrenaline pass through me, and I knew that the eclipse was over. I lunged every thing I had at Vesper with my telekinesis, and although it passed right through him, it distracted hi enough to give Destiny enough time to fly me and Julius out of there one at a time. After attempting to seal the hole with police tape back up in the surface, we ran to our Uber that we asked to wait and miraculously was still there. With sand blowing in my eyes, and pure adrenaline fueling my last steps, we collapsed into the vehicle, and Julius yelled at him to start driving.

As the car drifted past the pyramids and onto the road, I stared at the crystal in my hand. How much trouble we went through just to get a measly crystal. Everything in the last few days had led to this moment, and we did it! It wasn't a fail like the heist.

I grabbed my phone to text Axel, an although it was 1%, I saw something that made my hair stand on end.

6 missed calls from Axel, and 24 messages.

With my eyes widened, I opened my messages, and I could just barely make out the last message before my phone screen went black.

Don't come back.